Ka-chOWW!

By Ty Robinson
Illustrated by Todd Bright and Cristina Spagnoli
Designed by Tony Fejeran

Based on the characters and designs created by Pixar

Random House 🏠 New York

Library of Congress Control Number: 2007926734

ISBN: 978-0-7364-2404-2

www.randomhouse.com/kids/disney

MANUFACTURED IN CHINA

10 9 8 7 6 5 4 3 2

"**I** am speed!" McQueen chanted as he focused on the dirt track stretched out in front of him. "Is my pit crew ready?"

"Standing by," said Luigi. "Tires ready!"

"Pit stop!" Guido added happily.

VAAA-ROOOOM! McQueen revved his engine—and took off! "Woo-hooo!" he shouted. "It sure is great to zip around this dirt track after all that fancy stadium stuff. Out here, it's just me and—"

WHOOSH! "Whoa!" McQueen cried as he spun
out of control. He was headed toward a cactus patch!

"I give you the best tires, but look—you still wipe out,"
Luigi remarked as he stared down at McQueen.

"Yeah, thanks," McQueen replied. "Ouch! My turns work
perfectly on a real racetrack. Why can't I handle the dirt? I can't
wait till my racing stadium is built. I'll be cruising then!
Ka-chOWW! Ow-ow-OW!"

"I told ya to steer right to go left. Can't you remember anything, hotshot?" It was Doc. He had been watching the whole time!

"Hey, Doc," replied McQueen.
"What brings you out here, besides
grumbling about my racing style?"
"That's exactly why I'm here!"
Doc shouted back. "Mater, tow
your rookie friend out of this mess!"

"Hey, buddy!" called Mater. "I'll have you outta there faster than a runaway tractor slidin' on an oil slick!"

Sure enough, Mater got him up and out of the patch in a jiffy.

"I'm going back to town," McQueen grumbled.

"Now, wait just a second, rookie!" Doc challenged McQueen. "If I'm crew chief, you gotta do things my way. Plus you're on my turf!"

"Whatever," McQueen said. "But first can
I get cleaned up and take some of these prickles
out of my tires? I think I scratched my paint job—"
"No!" interrupted Doc. "Try that turn again—
unless it's too much for you, hotshot."

Reluctantly, McQueen stayed.

"New rules," lectured Doc. "No more worrying about your silly paint job. No more whining about a few cactus prickles. And no more rest until you make that turn look easy!"

McQueen tried the turn again . . .
and again . . . and again.
Sometimes he made it, and sometimes
he didn't. "Ow-ow-OW!" he shouted
each time he hit another cactus.

"I can do this, I know I can," McQueen said, revving his engine. "Watch me now."

Slowly, he returned to the starting line. Then, more determined than ever, he roared down the dirt track, concentrating on Doc's advice. And when he came to the curve, he glided around the corner—and stayed on the track!

"Ka-chow!" he hooted as he headed toward the finish line.
"Wahoo!" cried Mater. "You did it, buddy!"
"And with style!" added McQueen.

"Congratulations," said Doc. "You finally listened to some good advice."

"Yeah, the advice of a grumpy old car," McQueen spat back. Then he turned to Doc and grinned. "Feel like taking a little spin around the track?"

"Sure, rookie." Doc smiled and sped off. The race was on!

Ramone wasted no time. He happily went to work painting himself every color he could find.

"Good to see the old Ramone back!" shouted McQueen.

"You can say that again," Mater said, smiling. "In fact, I will. You can say that again!"

"Ramone, listen to me. If you want to paint yourself a new color, just go right ahead and do it."

"But I made a promise," Ramone said sadly.

"No, a happy, freshly painted Ramone made that promise," Flo said with a sigh. "I miss that Ramone. Just be yourself."

"Yeah," said Mater. "Just be yourself. We like ya that way." Ramone turned around. It seemed as if the whole town was there to encourage him.

Ramone stayed blue the next day and the next. He kept asking all the cars in town if they wanted paint jobs, but they were all too busy. Ramone couldn't stand it any longer. He had to paint something!

"Ramone! What's wrong with you, baby?" Flo said one day. But Ramone just shrugged and looked at his paint supplies.

"Looking sharp, soldier!" Sarge called out to Ramone.

"Thanks, Sarge," said Ramone. "Do you want a paint job? I haven't seen you in a different color in forever!"

"No, sir!" Sarge declared. "No time. I have to get my boot camp ready for when the customers come to town."

"Hey, baby, you want a quart of oil?" Flo asked Ramone.

"Yeah, thanks," Ramone said. Then he added, "Do you want me to give you a new paint job?"

"Oh, honey, thanks, but no," said Flo. "I have all this work to do."

The next day, Ramone got up early and started cleaning his shop to get ready for the customers who would soon be coming to town. But after a couple of hours, he was finished. He was tempted to paint himself a new color. Then he remembered his promise. So he went over to Flo's instead.

Ramone stopped short. "Hey, everybody! I've got an announcement to make!" he shouted. "In honor of Flo's birthday, I promise to stay blue for one full week!"

Everyone gasped. "Are you sure?" asked Flo.

"I'm surer than sure," Ramone replied.

Then Mater spoke up. "Hey, Ramone, do you think you can keep that promise you made to McQueen today?"

Ramone and Flo slowly cruised down Main Street
together as the rest of the cars watched.
"Oh, Ramone, this is a
wonderful birthday present," Flo said.

"Oh, Ramone!" Flo exclaimed. "You painted yourself blue!
You like it?" Ramone asked his wife.
"I sure do," Flo said, smiling. "It's still my favorite. Now, are
you going to take me on a birthday cruise or what?"

Suddenly, everyone stopped as they heard an engine revving. The door of Ramone's body shop popped open, and a very blue Ramone emerged, driving low and slow, with sparks trailing behind him.

That night, the whole town gathered for a neon cruise down Main Street in honor of Flo's birthday. But where was Ramone?

"Gee whiz!" shouted Mater. "I've never seen you stay one color for a whole week!"

"That's not a bad idea, there, Ramone," McQueen said. "You know, when I open my new headquarters in Radiator Springs, you'll have to paint someone besides yourself all day long."

"No problem," Ramone said, but McQueen wondered: How long could Ramone stay one color?

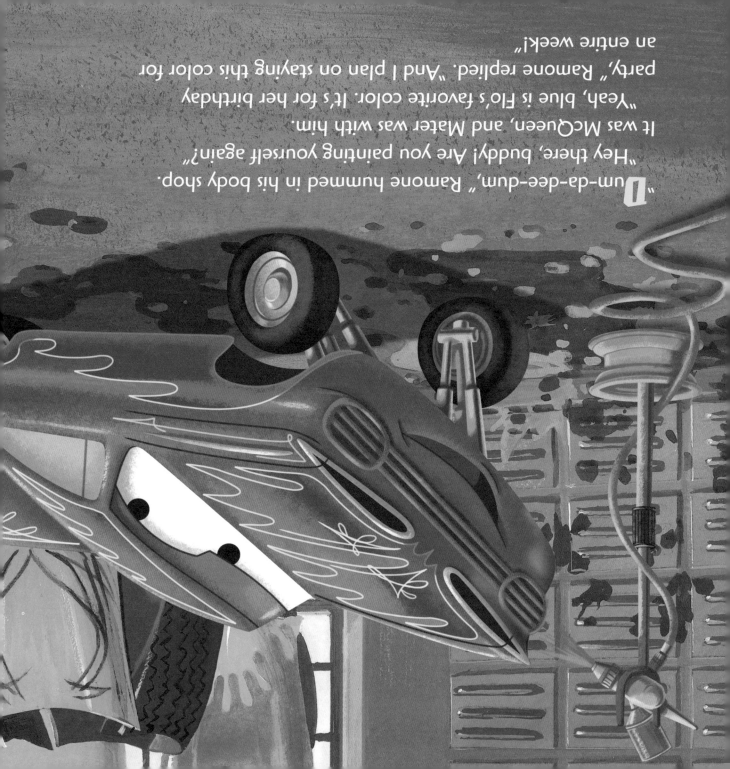

"Dum-da-dee-dum," Ramone hummed in his body shop.

"Hey there, buddy! Are you painting yourself again?" It was McQueen, and Mater was with him.

"Yeah, blue is Flo's favorite color. It's for her birthday party," Ramone replied. "And I plan on staying this color for an entire week!"

Blue Ramone

By Spencer Carson
Illustrated by Dan Gracey and Andrew Phillipson
Designed by Tony Fejeran

Based on the characters and designs created by Pixar

Random House 🏠 New York

Library of Congress Control Number: 2007926734

ISBN: 978-0-7364-2404-2

www.randomhouse.com/kids/disney

MANUFACTURED IN CHINA

10 9 8 7 6 5 4 3 2